The Bow-wow Bus

Read more Animal Inn books!

BOOK 1: A Furry Fiasco

BOOK 2: Treasure Hunt

Coming soon:

BOOK 4: Bright Lights, Big Kitty!

ANIMAL INN
The Bow-wow Bus

Book 3

PAUL DUBOIS JACOBS
&
JENNIFER SWENDER

Illustrated by STEPHANIE LABERIS

ALADDIN

New York London Toronto Sydney New Delhi

ALADDIN
An imprint of Simon & Schuster Children's Publishing Division
1230 Avenue of the Americas, New York, New York 10020
First Aladdin paperback edition April 2017

Also available in an Aladdin hardcover edition.

Cover designed by Jessica Handelman
Interior designed by Greg Stadnyk
The illustrations for this book were rendered digitally.
The text of this book was set in Bembo Std.
Manufactured in the United States of America 0317 OFF
2 4 6 8 10 9 7 5 3 1
Library of Congress Control Number 2016954218
ISBN 978-1-4814-6230-3 (hc)
ISBN 978-1-4814-6229-7 (pbk)
ISBN 978-1-4814-6231-0 (eBook)

For Annie W.

PROLOGUE

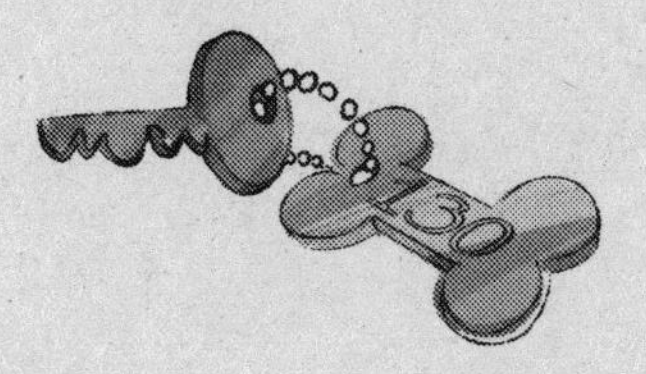

Beep-beep!

Beep-beep!

Yippee! The school bus is here.

Beep-beep!

Welcome to Animal Inn. My name is Coco. I'm a chocolate Labrador retriever.

No, I'm not made of chocolate, silly. I don't even like the stuff. We dogs aren't supposed to eat chocolate. But I do like to eat. Especially cheese.

I like cheddar cheese and Swiss cheese and American cheese.

I like cheese sticks and cheese balls and cheese puffs.

I like mac-and-cheese and grilled cheese and cheese pizza.

Luckily, my human sister, Cassie, likes cheese as much as I do. Cassie and I belong to the Tyler family. Our family includes five humans—Mom, Dad, Jake, Ethan, and Cassie—and seven pets:

- Me
- Dash—a Tibetan terrier
- Leopold—a scarlet macaw
- Shadow and Whiskers—sister and brother cats
- and Fuzzy and Furry—a pair of very adventurous gerbils

The Tylers used to live in an apartment in the city. Back then, Mom and Dad had two children, Jake and Ethan, and two pets, Dash and Leopold. But when Cassie and I came along, Mom and Dad bought this old house in the country.

Animal Inn is one part hotel, one part school, and one part spa. As our brochure says, *We promise to love your pet as much as you do.*

Beep-beep!

Where are Jake, Ethan, and Cassie? It's time for them to go to school.

Before long, customers will start to arrive. On some days, there is so much coming and going, Animal Inn could use a revolving door. We might have a Pekinese here for a pedicure. A Siamese for a short stay. Or a llama for a long stay.

On the first floor, we have the Welcome Area,

the office, the classroom, the grooming room, and my favorite—the party and play room.

Our family lives on the second floor. This includes Fuzzy and Furry snug in their gerbil-torium in Jake and Ethan's room.

The third floor is for smaller guests. We have a Reptile Room, a Rodent Room, and a Small Mammal Room. Larger guests stay out in the barn and kennels.

Beep-beep!

Where are those kids?

What if they miss the bus? What if they miss school?

School is so awesome. There's story time and lunchtime and playtime. In fact, just last week I got to spend an entire day with Cassie's first-grade class. Let me tell you what happened. . .

CHAPTER 1

It began like any other Monday.

When Cassie and I came downstairs that morning, Leopold was already on his perch. Dash sat nearby. Whiskers was curled up on the sofa, while Shadow hid behind it. (She likes to sneak outside whenever she gets the chance.)

Cassie was chattering to me as usual. "My school job this week is snack helper," she said. She unzipped her backpack and pulled out her lunch box. "Sit please, Princess Coco."

I sat. Cassie opened her lunch box and took out a little snack-pack filled with cubes of cheese. She gave one to me.

Yum. Cheddar.

"Now, if you have a question," Cassie said to me, "you need to raise your paw." She held up another piece of cheese. "Show me your paw, please."

I raised my paw.

"Very good, Princess Coco. But I won't be able to call you 'Princess,'" she said sadly. "In first grade, make-believe is only for recess and choice time. So in class, I will just call you Coco."

Cassie backed up a few steps and patted her thighs. "Come, Coco," she called.

I trotted over and nudged her hand with my

nose. She gave me another piece of cheese.

"Now for the fun part," Cassie said. She went to the supply closet and found her old backpack from preschool—the one that looks like a ladybug. I'd worn Cassie's ladybug backpack before, like the time we ran away to the barn.

Dash looked at Leopold. Leopold looked at Dash. Whiskers looked a little nervous. But I was curious. What was Cassie up to now?

"Sit please, Princess Coco. I mean, just Coco."

I sat.

"Show me your paw, Coco."

I raised a paw. Cassie held it in her hand. She gently guided my paw through the shoulder strap of the backpack. Then she guided my other paw through the other strap. The backpack was a little wobbly, so Cassie tightened it up.

"Cassie!" Mom called from upstairs. "Did you remember to brush your teeth?"

"Oops," Cassie said. "I'll be right back," she whispered to me. "You stay here." She tossed me another cube of cheese. She put the snack-pack back into her lunch box and set it next to the sofa. Then she ran up the stairs.

I plopped down on the floor. Whew! That was a lot of activity for so early in the morning.

Shadow came out from her hiding spot behind the sofa. "What's with the ladybug?" she asked me. "Are you and Cassie running away again?"

"Don't be silly," I said. "It's a school day."

"Then why are you wearing a backpack?" asked Whiskers.

"Cassie put it there," I said.

"We know that," said Shadow. "But *why*?"

"It appears Cassie is bringing Coco to school today," said Dash.

"I agree," said Leopold. "Weekly job assignment. Question protocol. Make-believe-play rules."

"Well, I'm glad *I'm* not the one going to school," said Whiskers.

"I am not going to school," I said. I stretched out in my sunny spot. "I am going to take a nap."

CHAPTER 2

Jake, Ethan, and Cassie ran downstairs.

"Cassie, why is Coco wearing your ladybug backpack?" Jake asked.

"Are you running away to the barn again?" said Ethan.

"No, silly," answered Cassie. "It's a school day."

"Boys!" Dad called from upstairs. "Did you remember to feed Fuzzy and Furry?"

"Ethan fed them," Jake answered.

"I didn't feed them," said Ethan. "I thought you fed them."

"It's your turn," said Jake.

"I thought it was your turn," said Ethan.

The boys dropped their backpacks and ran upstairs, almost bumping into Mom and Dad, who were on their way down.

"Cassie," said Mom, "are you all set for show-and-tell today?"

Cassie nodded. She unzipped her backpack and pulled out a dog show ribbon. "I'm going to show this," she said.

The ribbon was purple and shiny. In fancy gold letters, it said *1st Place.*

Cassie came over to me and held the ribbon to my collar.

"Coco is going to be my show dog," she said. "I am going to *show* her for show-and-tell."

"But, sweetheart," said Dad, "you can't bring Coco to school."

"I'm afraid Dad is right," said Mom. "Coco has to stay home today."

"But I told everyone they would get to meet Coco," said Cassie. "I told Helena and Mattias and Lucy and Seiji and Arlen and Laura." She reluctantly took off my ladybug backpack.

I didn't like to see Cassie sad. I nuzzled her with my nose. I wanted her to know that I was just fine staying home.

"I have an idea," said Dad. He leaned down and whispered something into Cassie's ear. Cassie's sad face suddenly turned into a happy face.

"I can't believe it!" Cassie squealed excitedly. "Do you really think so?"

"It can't hurt to ask," said Dad. "I'll call the school this morning."

Beep-beep!

Beep-beep!

"Jake! Ethan!" Mom called upstairs. "The bus is here."

The boys hurried down, picked up their backpacks, and rushed out the front door. Cassie gave me a big hug and stuffed the ribbon into her backpack. Then she skipped out the door after the boys. Mom and Dad followed.

"I can't believe it!" I heard Cassie squeal again. "Now my whole class will get to meet *all* my pets!"

CHAPTER 3

"What did Cassie just say?" Whiskers asked with concern.

"I believe she said, *Now my whole class will get to meet all my pets,*" said Leopold. He even sounded like Cassie. Leopold is very good at repeating things.

"We're *all* going to school?" said Whiskers. "I just want to stay on my sofa."

"Let's not get ahead of ourselves," said Dash.

"We can't believe everything we hear from Cassie. Remember what happened with Miss KD?"

Miss KD was a Komodo dragon who bunked in our basement. There were a lot of misunderstandings before she arrived. We overheard Cassie say a wizard was coming to Animal Inn. But the "wizard" turned out to be a *lizard*.

"And let's not forget the incident with the pirate," said Leopold.

Not long ago, we overheard Cassie say a harbor pirate was coming to Animal Inn. But the harbor "pirate" turned out to be a harbor *pilot* named Annie. It didn't help that Annie's dog was called Blackbeard, just like the famous buccaneer.

"But you heard her," said Whiskers. "Cassie said her whole class will get to meet all her pets. Right, Shadow?"

Shadow didn't answer. Where was she?

"Excuse me," said a tiny voice. "I used to be in a school."

It was Blub.

Blub is a goldfish who was dropped off at Animal Inn a few weeks ago. Blub's owner went on a short business trip that turned into a long business trip that turned into an even longer business trip. In the meantime, Blub stayed in a fishbowl in the Welcome Area. It was just temporary, until his owner came back for him.

"I liked my school," continued Blub. "Fresh Pond Elementary. I had lots of friends. There was Goldie and Bubbles and Finn. I was even on the swim team." Blub swam a quick lap around his bowl.

I was about to ask Blub more about his school, when Mom and Dad came back from walking

the kids to the bus stop. They both seemed very excited.

"I'll call Cassie's teacher, Mr. C., right now," said Dad.

"I think this is a great idea," said Mom. She and Dad made their way to the office.

Dash looked at Leopold. Leopold looked at Dash.

Maybe we were going to school after all. But before I could give it another thought, I noticed the scent of cheese. I followed it to . . . Cassie's lunch box?

"Not again," I said. I picked up the lunch box in my mouth. The handle didn't taste very good.

Ding-dong!

Mom hurried out of the office. "What've you got there, Coco?" she asked. "Oh no. Did Cassie forget her lunch again?"

Mom took the lunch box from me and patted my head. Then she opened the front door. It was Sierra, our college intern.

"Good morning," said Mom.

"Good morning," said Sierra. "Look who I found outside." Sierra had her bike helmet under one arm and Shadow under the other.

"Shadow, you little sneak," said Mom.

Shadow skittered back behind the sofa.

I walked over to Sierra and sniffed her bag.

"Coco," Mom said with a laugh, "that's not polite."

"It's okay," said Sierra. "She knows I have treats in here." Sierra always brings us treats, like Doggie Donuts and Kitty Krisps. Yum.

I sat down at Sierra's feet and wagged my tail. She reached into her bag and pulled out a Doggie Donut. She tossed it in the air.

I caught it. It was cheese-and-bacon-flavored! Double yum.

"How's my favorite sofa-surfer?" Sierra asked Whiskers. She placed a Kitty Krisp next to him. Whiskers actually started purring.

Sierra tossed another Kitty Krisp behind the

sofa for Shadow. She gave a Doggie Donut to Dash and a seed pop to Leopold.

"And . . . ," Sierra said with a smile. She reached deeper into her bag. "I even remembered a treat for Blub today." She walked over and sprinkled a handful of colorful flakes into Blub's bowl.

Sierra touched her fingertip to the surface of the water. Blub gently bumped it with his nose. "Goldfish high-five!" she cheered. "Any word from Blub's owner?" she asked Mom.

"Just got an e-mail," said Mom. "It looks like Blub might be with us for a while yet."

"Well, what's the plan for this morning?" asked Sierra.

"The Rodent Room and Small Mammal Room need some attention," said Mom.

"Hi, Sierra," said Dad, coming out of the office.

"Did you reach Mr. C.?" Mom asked Dad.

"Yes, great news. He loves the idea."

We animals perked up our ears.

"What idea?" asked Sierra.

"The pets are going to visit with Cassie's class," said Mom. "Do you think you might be able to help out?"

"It shouldn't be a problem," said Sierra. "When's the visit?"

"That's the best part," Dad said excitedly. He started following Mom and Sierra up the stairs. "It's *tomorrow*!"

CHAPTER 4

"Tomorrow?" Whiskers said nervously.

Shadow emerged from behind the sofa, still chomping on her treat. "What's going on tomorrow?" she asked, her mouth full of crumbs.

"It appears we are all going to school," said Leopold.

"Sounds cool," said Shadow. "What are we doing there?"

"Not sure," said Dash. "But I know how we can find out. Follow me to the gerbiltorium."

We all hurried upstairs to Jake and Ethan's room. Fuzzy and Furry were lounging in one of their play structures.

"Greetings, friends," said Fuzzy.

"Care for a snack?" added Furry. He was nibbling on a cashew.

"No thanks," said Dash. "We've got a job for you and we need to hurry."

"Speed is our specialty," said Fuzzy.

"But it's an additional charge," added Furry.

"I believe after what happened last time," said Leopold, "this job should be for free."

For their last job, Fuzzy and Furry were

supposed to print an e-mail from the computer in the office. Instead, they ordered a framed photo of themselves. Mom and Dad are still trying to figure out where it came from.

"Point taken," said Fuzzy.

"Give us the lowdown," added Furry.

"Lucky for us, Cassie forgot her lunch box again," said Dash. "Mom or Dad will have to bring it to school, and you two are going to hide inside it."

"When you get to Cassie's classroom," Leopold added, "sneak out and investigate."

"We need all the information you can find about pets going to school," said Dash.

"You got it," said Fuzzy. "Except . . ."

"Except what?" asked Shadow.

"The plan will never work," added Furry.

"Why not?" asked Dash.

"How do we get home?" asked Fuzzy.

"We're not exactly flying squirrels," added Furry.

"I hadn't thought about that," said Dash. He looked at Leopold. Leopold shrugged.

"I have an idea," I said.

"I can't wait to hear this," said Shadow. "Does it involve cheese?"

"No, silly," I said. "What if Fuzzy and Furry stay at school for the whole day? Then they can sneak back into Cassie's lunch box and take the school bus home with the kids."

"That's quite brilliant," said Leopold.

"They'll have plenty of time," said Dash.

"Are we sure these two rodents can handle school?" asked Shadow.

"See this?" said Fuzzy, holding up a cashew.

"Brain food," added Furry.

They giggled and picked the lock on the gerbiltorium. Then they scurried into the heating vent and disappeared.

CHAPTER 5

By the time we got back to the Welcome Area, Fuzzy and Furry were already inside the lunch box. It wiggled ever so slightly.

Dad came down from the third floor. "I'm taking Cassie's lunch box to school," he called upstairs. "Be right back."

Dad picked up the lunch box. "Sure feels like a

big lunch," he said on his way out the door. If he only knew.

I stretched out in my sunny spot. There was nothing to do now but wait. "I hope Cassie didn't miss lunchtime," I said.

"Lunchtime is usually at noon," said Whiskers matter-of-factly. "Recess is generally right after lunch. Then dismissal is at about three o'clock."

"How do you know so much about school?" I asked.

"Don't you remember, Coco?" said Shadow. "Whiskers and I lived in a schoolyard when we were kittens."

"I didn't like it," said Whiskers. "One time, there was a fire drill. The alarm was so loud."

"Come on, Little Brother," said Shadow. "It

wasn't that bad. We had a place to sleep under the play structure and all the cafeteria leftovers we could eat."

"But it was cold in the winter," said Whiskers. "And we didn't have a family."

I still remember the day Shadow and Whiskers arrived at Animal Inn. I was just a pup then. We hadn't been open very long when a nice man named Mr. Raymond showed up at the front door with a cardboard box. Shadow and Whiskers were inside. They were so cute.

"Well, it all turned out for the best," I said.

"I still didn't like it," said Whiskers.

"I liked my school," said Blub, in his tiny voice. "We played lots of games, like Fishy, Fishy, Cross My Ocean and Go Fish!" Blub sighed. Small bubbles floated to the top of his bowl.

"I liked my school too," said Dash. "When I was young, I went to a show dog academy. We learned lots of important skills."

"What about you, Leopold?" I asked. "Have you ever been to school?"

"I'm what you might call homeschooled," said Leopold. "I've learned everything I know right here."

"Me too!" I said. "I learned how to read in the Furry Pages. I started with beginner books, like *Go, Dog. Go!* But now I can read chapter books, like Henry and Mudge, with a little help."

Every Saturday, Dad and Jake host a class called the Furry Pages, where children read aloud to an animal buddy. I love the Furry Pages. If Cassie's class was anything like that, we had nothing to worry about.

"I think school will be fun," I said.

Ding-dong!

Mom came downstairs to open the door. It was Martha, the Animal Inn groomer.

"Good morning, everybody," said Martha.

"Hi, Martha," said Mom. "Listen, we need to add a few customers to your schedule today. The Tyler pets all need a brush and a trim."

"No problem," said Martha. "What's the occasion?"

"School visit," said Mom, heading for the stairs.

"Sounds exciting," said Martha.

Ding-dong!

"I'll get it," called Martha. She opened the front door. It was our good friend Sheila the shar-pei, here for a shampoo.

"Hello, cuddly Coco," Sheila whispered as she passed by. "Nice to see you, wonderful Whiskers.

Good morning, darling Dash. Greetings, lovely Leopold. What's new, shimmering Shadow? Hi there, beautiful Blub."

Sheila followed Martha into the grooming room.

"Get ready, Whiskers," Martha called back to the Welcome Area. "You're next!"

CHAPTER 6

"Who knew hamsters could make such a mess?" said Mom, coming down the stairs. She wiped her arm across her brow.

"They do like to hide food in funny places," said Sierra.

Ding-dong!

Mom answered the door.

"Hello," said a man. "I'm Andrew Patel, and this

is my new dog, Lucky. He'll be staying with you for a few days."

"Yes, we're expecting you," said Mom. "Welcome to Animal Inn."

Lucky was a medium-size hound dog. I love meeting new friends. I walked over to say hello.

Woof-woof-woof-woof-woof!

Lucky barked and barked.

"I'm afraid Lucky's not that good with other dogs," Mr. Patel said over the loud barking. "He's a rescue pup."

Woof-woof-woof-woof-woof!

"Maybe a treat would help," said Sierra. She slowly walked over to Lucky. Then she bent down and offered him a Doggie Donut. "Here you go, my friend," she said calmly.

Lucky took the treat.

"It's yummy, right?" I whispered to him.

Lucky nodded and lay down at Sierra's feet, chewing happily.

"That's amazing," said Mr. Patel. "Lucky can get a little nervous, but he calmed right down with you. You're so good with him."

"Yes, Sierra is our incredible intern," said Mom. "Why don't you go ahead and give Lucky to her. She can get him settled in his kennel."

"I'll bring Coco, too," said Sierra. She grabbed my leash from the hook by the door. "Looks like Lucky could use a friend."

"Bye, Lucky," said Mr. Patel, reaching down to pat his head. "Be a good dog. I'll be back for you soon. It's only for a few days."

Sierra, Lucky, and I headed outside. It felt good to get a little fresh air.

"I'm Coco," I whispered to Lucky. "Welcome to Animal Inn. You'll like it here. We promise to love you as much as your owner does."

"Which one?" Lucky asked.

"What do you mean?" I said.

"Which owner?" said Lucky. "My first owner moved to a new apartment and couldn't have a dog. He gave me back to the shelter. My second owner didn't have time for a puppy. So she gave me back to the shelter. My third owner turned out to be allergic to dogs. He gave me back to the shelter. Mr. Patel is my fourth owner. Lucky is my fourth name. And now Mr. Patel's leaving me here," he said sadly.

"It's only for a few days," I offered.

"That's what my last owner told me." Lucky said.

Sierra slid open the barn door. Today our only barn guest was an Angora goat named Toni. She was so fluffy.

"Hi, Toni," I said as we passed by. "This is Lucky."

"Pleased to meet you, Lucky," said Toni.

Sierra walked us to the back of the barn and opened the door to the kennels. She got Lucky settled in his enclosure and gave him a whole handful of Doggie Donuts. She filled his water bowl and fluffed up the dog bed in the corner. Then she opened the door to his outside run.

"Your owner will be back for you soon," I whispered to Lucky. "I'm sure of it."

CHAPTER 7

When we got back to the Welcome Area, Sierra hung up my leash. Then she went to find Mom.

Sheila the shar-pei was just leaving. She looked very stylish.

"Toodle-loo, cuddly Coco," Sheila whispered as she followed Martha to the door. "Always a pleasure, wonderful Whiskers. See you, darling

Dash. So long, lovely Leopold. Are you back there, shimmering Shadow? Bye-bye, beautiful Blub."

"You're next, my dear," Martha said to Whiskers. She gently picked him up off the sofa and carried him back to the grooming room. Whiskers did not look happy.

"How's Lucky doing?" asked Dash.

"Okay," I said. "Did you know that he's had *four* families? His owners keep giving him away."

"Poor chap," said Leopold.

"I'm just happy we don't have to worry about that," I said. I settled down on the floor and closed my eyes. Even dogs like catnaps.

When Martha brought Whiskers out a little while later, his coat was brushed and very shiny.

"You look handsome," I whispered to Whiskers.

"I need to clean up the room a bit," Martha said. "Then it's your turn, Shadow."

"Humph," I heard from behind the sofa.

Just then, the front door opened. Dad was back. "I'm home," he said.

"How did it go?" Mom called from the party and play room.

"Great," said Dad, going to join Mom. "Everyone will be included."

Included in what? I wondered. I sure hoped Fuzzy and Furry came back with some answers.

Suddenly, we heard a loud voice. "Can I please have your attention? Would Dash Tyler, Leopold Tyler, Coco Tyler, Shadow Tyler, and Whiskers Tyler report to the principal's office."

"Immediately!" said another voice.

We all froze. Even Dash and Leopold looked a little nervous.

Then we heard a giggle. And another giggle. Fuzzy popped out of the heating vent with a grin. Furry followed close behind.

"Did we get your attention?" asked Fuzzy.

"Just a little something we heard at school," added Furry.

"I thought the plan was for you to take the bus home," I said.

"Dad ended up chatting with Cassie's teacher for a while," said Fuzzy.

"We had plenty of time," added Furry.

"What did you find out?" asked Dash.

"Brace yourselves," said Fuzzy.

"Stay strong," added Furry.

"The entire school . . . ," said Fuzzy.

"Is nut free!" added Furry.

"Well, there were a least two nuts there," snickered Shadow.

"And we saw a poster," said Fuzzy.

"For a gigantic spelling bee," added Furry.

"Imagine," said Fuzzy. "A gigantic bee."

"That can *spell*!" added Furry.

"My dear friends," said Leopold, "a spelling bee is a competition, not an insect."

"That's right," said Dash. "It's nothing to worry about."

"Then worry about this!" said Fuzzy. "We heard Denise, the school nurse, talking. One of the kids has a bug. . . ."

"In her tummy!" added Furry.

"Guys, focus," said Dash. "What about Cassie's

classroom? Did you find anything there?"

"They have an aquarium," said Fuzzy.

"It is very soothing," added Furry.

"None of this information is very helpful," said Shadow.

"I have to agree," said Leopold. "Was there anything else?"

"Yes," said Fuzzy. "We saw Cassie's teacher throw this into the recycling bin." Fuzzy pulled a small square of folded paper out of the heating vent.

"It's part of a note," added Furry, "going home in folders today."

"I can read it," I said.

Fuzzy and Furry worked together to unfold the strip of paper. Then they ran back and forth to smooth it out.

"'Dear First-Grade Families,'" I read aloud.

"'Please join us tomorrow (yes, TOMORROW!) as we meet the pets of Animal Inn. We will be . . .'"

"We will be . . . We will be . . . what?" asked Whiskers.

"That's all it says," I told him. "The page is torn."

"Figures," said Shadow. "I knew I should have gone with them."

"What now?" I asked.

Dash looked at Leopold. Leopold looked at Dash. "We're not sure," they both said at the same time.

"Well, I plan to be absent," grumbled Whiskers.

"But being part of a school is fun," said a tiny voice. It was Blub again.

I padded over to his bowl. "Do you think you can join us tomorrow, Blub?" I asked.

"I'd better stay here in case my owner comes to pick me up," he gurgled.

"He'll be back for you soon," I whispered.

I had just said the same thing to Lucky. I sure hoped I was right.

CHAPTER 8

"Shadow," called Martha, "it's your turn."

Shadow darted behind the sofa.

"Look what Sierra gave me," said Martha. "Your favorite." Martha sprinkled a line of Kitty Krisps on the floor.

"Too . . . yummy . . . to . . . resist," Shadow

whispered between mouthfuls. Martha quickly scooped her up.

"Drat," Shadow muttered as she was carried away.

When Shadow returned a little while later,

she wore a new collar with a tinkling bell. "Now everybody will know where I am," she huffed under her breath.

"Coco, your turn," said Martha. "Dash is on deck. And last, but certainly not least, will be Leopold."

Martha gave me the works—bath, brush, and blow dry. I love the smell of Martha's shampoos.

When I was finished, Martha walked me back to the Welcome Area. I found a sunny spot and settled down for an afternoon nap. I soon fell into the strangest dream.

All the pets were there. I was driving the bus to school, but I didn't know which way to go. Fuzzy and Furry said they could help with directions. They would be my GPS—Gerbil Positioning System.

Whiskers kept telling me to slow down, but Shadow kept telling me to go faster. Dash and Leopold were leaning out the open window, enjoying the wind in their fur and feathers. Driving the bus was so cool! *Vroom! Vroom! Vroom!*

"Wake up, Princess Coco," Cassie said in a soft voice. "Wake up."

I slowly opened my eyes. I saw Mom and Dad and Jake and Ethan and Cassie. The kids were home from school! I wagged my tail.

"Hi, Dash," said Jake.

"Hi, Leopold," said Ethan. "You guys look nice."

"Shadow and Whiskers look great too," said Jake.

"I love Shadow's new bell!" cheered Cassie.

"Everyone is spiffed up and ready for the visit tomorrow," said Mom.

"And listen to this," Dad said. "Mr. C. and I had an idea. Animal Inn is going to donate a pet to the class."

"What does 'donate' mean?" asked Cassie.

I was glad she asked, because I didn't know either. I was hoping "donate" had something to do with "donuts."

"It means to give," said Ethan.

"More specifically, it means to give *away*," said Jake. "Like a present."

What? Give away a pet?

"I think it's a great idea," said Mom.

She did?

"And I know just the pet," said Dad.

He did? Was I still dreaming?

"My school friends are going to love my animal friends," said Cassie. "Shadow, you are going to love Lucy. She might even scoop you up and take you home with her."

What? Was Cassie going to let Lucy take Shadow?

Cassie skipped over to Dash. "Dash, you and Helena are both very helpful. And Helena always wanted a dog."

Was Cassie going to give Dash to Helena?

"Leopold, you are going to love Mattias," continued Cassie. "Mattias won the first-grade spelling bee."

So it *was* a spelling bee and not a bumblebee. At least *that* was good news.

But how could the Tylers give Leopold away?

"Whiskers, you and Seiji are going to be fast friends," Cassie said. "Seiji gets a little nervous too. He'll take good care of you."

Was Seiji going to take Whiskers?

Then Cassie skipped over to me. "And Mr. C. will just love you, Coco. He loves anything chocolate. He might just eat you up."

Gulp!

"Who's ready for a snack?" asked Mom.

Jake, Ethan, and Cassie raced upstairs. Mom and Dad followed.

Usually, I followed too. Cassie always shared her afterschool snack with me. But this time, I stayed just where I was.

I had lost my appetite.

CHAPTER 9

"Are they really giving one of us to Cassie's class?" I asked.

"Donating," said Leopold.

"It's the same thing," Whiskers insisted.

"Let's slow down," said Dash. "What exactly did Dad say?"

"I'm afraid I heard the same as Coco," said

Leopold. "Animal Inn will donate a pet to Cassie's class."

"And Dad knows just the pet," I said sadly.

"Who do you think it is?" asked Whiskers.

"Well, we know it's not Dash," said Shadow. "Dash is a dog-show champion. And Mom's had him for, like, a million years."

"I'm not that old," said Dash.

"I doubt it could be me," said Leopold, nervously preening his feathers. "I believe a macaw is too sophisticated a pet for your average first grader."

"Well, it can't be me," said Shadow. "You can't have an outdoor cat as a classroom pet."

"But I'm an indoor cat," Whiskers whimpered.

"Calm down, Little Brother," said Shadow. "Mom and Dad would never separate us."

If it wasn't Dash or Leopold or Shadow or Whiskers, that left . . . me.

Just then, Fuzzy and Furry popped out of the heating vent.

"We hear Shadow has a new collar," said Fuzzy.

"We can literally hear it," added Furry.

"Very funny," said Shadow. She tried to shake the collar loose, but it only made the little bell ring more. "Drat," she muttered.

"Could it be Fuzzy or Furry?" Whiskers asked.

"Could what be Fuzzy?" asked Fuzzy.

"Or Furry?" added Furry.

"Mom and Dad are giving one of us away to Cassie's class," I said.

"But we're Jake and Ethan's pets," said Fuzzy.

"We're not Mom and Dad's to give," added Furry.

"Well, it's not going to be me!" cried Whiskers.

"What are we going to do?" I asked. I didn't care how much Mr. C. loved chocolate things. I didn't want to be given away. I didn't want a new family.

"Maybe they meant temporarily," said Fuzzy.

"Like only for a few days," added Furry.

Gulp!

That's exactly what Lucky's last owner had said.

CHAPTER 10

That night, I couldn't sleep. Usually I feel safe and cozy, snuggled at the foot of Cassie's bed. Instead, I tossed and turned. Would the Tylers really give one of us away?

I could hear Leopold in his sleeping cage in the corner of the room. He was talking in his sleep. It sounded like he was having a bad dream.

I wondered about Dash at the foot of Jake's

bed, and Shadow and Whiskers in Mom and Dad's rocking chair. Were they as worried and confused as I was?

When I came downstairs the next morning, the other pets were already in the Welcome Area. It didn't look like anyone had slept well.

Cassie, on the other hand, seemed to have slept just fine. But something was odd. She didn't have her backpack and she was still in her pajamas, the footie ones covered in dancing lambs.

"I can't believe it, Princess Coco!" Cassie sang. She skipped over to me and tickled me behind the ears. Then she bounced over to the sofa and plopped down next to Whiskers.

"I just can't believe it!" Cassie sang again. She held Whiskers's front paws and did a little dance. Whiskers did not look happy.

“Leopold,” Cassie said with a smile, “can you believe it?”

“Leopold cannot believe it,” Leopold squawked from his perch. Cassie had taught him that.

“This is going to be the best day ever!” cheered Cassie, giving Dash a hug.

"Cassie!" Mom called from upstairs. "You still need to brush your teeth, even if you're not going to school."

"Coming!" sang Cassie. She ran back up the stairs.

"Cassie's not going to school today?" Whiskers asked.

"I hope not," said Shadow, stepping out from behind the sofa. "Not in those lambie jammies."

"At this rate, she'll never make it to the bus on time," said Leopold.

Just then, Jake and Ethan came downstairs. Mom and Dad followed. Mom was carrying a big cardboard box. It looked heavy.

"Ethan, did you feed Fuzzy and Furry?" asked Jake.

"Uh, yeah," said Ethan. "I did."

"Oh," said Jake, a bit surprised. "Good."

"I'll walk you to the bus stop," said Dad. "I'm heading out to do the morning chores in the barn and kennels."

"Please give Lucky a little extra attention," said Mom, trying to balance the box in her arms. "He still seems a bit gloomy."

"Will do," said Dad.

Beep-beep!

Beep-beep!

"You better hurry, boys," said Mom. "Have a great day." Then she carried the box to the party and play room.

"Cassie must be staying home sick today," said Whiskers. "I couldn't be happier."

"You're happy that Cassie is sick?" I asked.

"I'm not happy that she's sick," Whiskers

explained. "I'm happy that she's not going to school."

"Cassie does not appear to be sick," said Leopold.

"When Cassie's sick, we stay in bed and listen to an audiobook," I said. "Mom gives us warm milk and crackers."

"I know," Shadow piped up. "It's a teacher meeting day. Those teachers are always having meetings."

"Then why did Jake and Ethan go to school?" Dash asked.

"They all attend the same school," said Leopold.

"All that matters," said Whiskers, "is that Cassie is not going to school. That means *we* are not going to school. That means I can stay right here in peace." He snuggled down into the sofa cushions.

I thought for a moment. "If no pets are going to school," I said, "then no pets can be given away to the class."

I took a deep breath. Everything was back to normal.

At least, I hoped.

CHAPTER 11

Beep-beep!

Beep-beep!

"Yippee!" cheered Cassie. "The bus is here!"

Cassie had changed out of her jammies and was now wearing her Animal Inn T-shirt and a pair of jeans. She ran out the front door. Mom and Dad followed close behind.

"Why is the bus back?" Whiskers asked nervously.

"This is highly unusual," said Leopold.

Fuzzy and Furry skittered out of the heating vent.

"There's a big yellow bus outside!" announced Fuzzy.

"We spied it from the crow's nest," added Furry.

"You're a little late," said Shadow, slinking out from behind the sofa.

"Well, there's a lot of them," said Fuzzy.

"I counted twenty-five," added Furry.

"Twenty-five!" cried Whiskers

"Twenty-five what?" asked Dash.

Before the gerbils could answer, the front door swung open.

Fuzzy and Furry disappeared into the heating vent. Whiskers buried his head under a cushion. Shadow scampered behind the sofa. And Dash,

Leopold, and I braced ourselves. Into the Welcome Area came . . . *Sierra?*

"Good morning, my furry and feathered friends." She hung her bike helmet next to the leashes. "Are you ready?" she asked. "Because here comes . . ."

Cassie?

Cassie was followed by lots and lots of children, not to mention a few grown-ups, including Mom and Dad. Everyone crowded into the Welcome Area.

Cassie led me to a man holding a clipboard. "Mr. C., this is Coco," she said. "Coco, this is my teacher, Mr. C."

The man smiled at me. "I've heard so much about you, Coco," he said.

Then Cassie ran to stand on the bottom step.

Animal
Inn

"Welcome to Animal Inn," she cheered, "where we promise to love your pet as much as you do."

"Boys and girls," said Mr. C., "let's put on our best listening ears."

"How many of you have a pet at home?" Dad asked the students.

Several children raised their hands.

"Wonderful," said Mom. "Today you'll get a chance to meet the pets of Animal Inn."

Helena raised her hand. "I have a question," she said.

I had a question too. Was one of us still going to be . . . what was that word again?

Donated.

CHAPTER 12

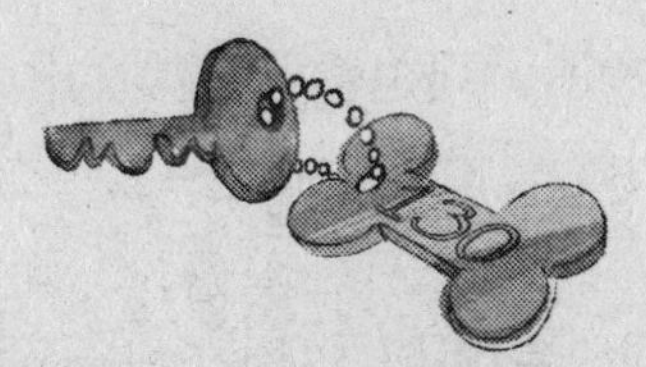

Everyone made their way to the party and play room. I chose a carpet square next to Seiji. Cassie had said that Seiji could get a little nervous. Maybe we could help each other. I was feeling a little nervous too.

I turned in a circle, pawed at my carpet square, and then plopped down. I tried to get comfy. No use. I still felt nervous.

"Our first family pet was Dash," Mom told the class. She called Dash to the front of the room. "Dash is a Tibetan terrier."

Dash showed the class some tricks, like high-five and roll over.

"Now let's meet Leopold," said Dad. "His full name is Leopold Augustus Gonzalo Tyler. He's a scarlet macaw."

"Leopold is a pretty bird," squawked Leopold. "No, Leopold cannot believe it." Everyone laughed. Leopold took a bow.

"Our next pet is Coco," said Mom.

Cassie bounced over to my carpet square and gave me a big hug. "Coco is a chocolate Lab, but her favorite food is cheese," said Cassie.

"And all these pets love to listen to children read," said Dad.

"Yay!" cheered the children. "Let's read!"

Mom brought over the big cardboard box. She reached inside and took out a handful of books. She, Dad, and Sierra started passing them out to the children.

Hey, this was feeling just like Furry Pages. And I love Furry Pages.

I looked over at Dash. He was sitting in the middle of three children who were taking turns reading to him. Leopold was on his perch, paying close attention to a chapter book Mr. C. was reading aloud to a small group in the corner.

I took a deep breath. We had nothing to worry about. I was even getting my appetite back and my tummy told me it must be close to snack time.

Luckily, there were apple slices, crackers, and . . . *cheese*! Seiji gave me a piece of his. Yum.

After reading time, the class headed upstairs for a tour. We passed by the gerbiltorium to say hello to Fuzzy and Furry. How did they get hold of an apple slice?

We then went to the Reptile Room on the third floor. The turtle and snake enclosures didn't have any guests at the moment, but the children still enjoyed seeing the habitats.

We moved on to the Rodent Room, where there were two hamsters named Jackson and Wolfie, and a chinchilla named Morris. The children helped fill the food bowls and water bottles. Sierra told them a few fun facts about each animal. I didn't know that hamsters could store food in their cheeks. That was like having a snack-pack in your mouth.

In the Small Mammal Room, we met two checkered giant rabbits named Socks and Boots. Mom and Dad had the children sit in a circle. Then Sierra lifted the rabbits out of their hutch. She put them in the middle of the floor for a little bunny exercise.

It turned out Whiskers was correct. Lunch was right at noon. We all headed outside for a picnic.

Cassie's classmates were very generous with their sandwich crusts. Mom and Dad passed out cups of homemade lemonade. (I had water.)

And recess was right after lunch. The children's favorite game was Fishy, Fishy, Cross My Ocean. It was so much fun! I could see why this was Blub's favorite game.

After we cooled off and caught our breath, it was time to visit the barn and kennels. Everybody loved Toni the Angora goat, but Toni seemed a little concerned.

"Are there enough stalls for all these new guests?" she asked me.

"Oh, they're not guests," I said. "They're first graders."

Toni nodded. She looked relieved.

Before opening the door to the kennels, Mom

asked the children to be extra quiet. "We have a new guest named Lucky," she explained. "It's his first time here and he's a little homesick."

Lucky was resting on his bed. He still looked sad. I sure hoped his owner was coming back for him soon.

Finally, we returned to the party and play room for some coloring pages and crossword puzzles. One clue asked: *Which Animal Inn pet is the color of chocolate, but loves cheese? Four letters.*

I snuggled on my carpet square. I didn't feel nervous anymore. Just tired. School was a lot of fun, but it could sure tucker you out.

CHAPTER 13

The class gathered in the Welcome Area to wait for the bus back to school. Mr. C. asked for everyone's attention. I made sure to put on my best listening ears.

"We need to thank Animal Inn for such a wonderful field trip," he said.

The children applauded.

"But the fun doesn't end here," said Mr. C.

It doesn't? I thought.

"Cassie's family has very kindly offered to donate one of the Animal Inn pets to our classroom."

"Yay!" The children all cheered.

Dash looked at Leopold. Leopold looked at Dash. Whiskers jumped into Seiji's lap.

In the middle of all the games and excitement and new friends, I had thought we were safe.

I noticed Dad walk toward Leopold's perch. It couldn't be Leopold. Could it?

"Here, Dash," called Mom. Was it Dash? How could it be Dash?

Then Cassie walked over to the sofa. Oh no! Was it Whiskers? Or was Cassie looking for Shadow?

Where was Shadow, anyway? I hadn't seen her all day.

"Coco," Mom said, looking straight at me.

Gulp!

"Coco," Mom said again.

I couldn't believe what was happening!

"Coco, could you move over a little? Thanks."

Whew! I breathed a sigh of relief.

Mom walked past me and over to Blub's bowl.

"I'm sure your class will take excellent care of Blub until his owner returns for him," she said.

"And I think he'll be much happier in that beautiful aquarium in your classroom," said Dad.

"We are honored to have Blub join our school," said Mr. C.

"Yippee!" I heard Blub bubble happily. "I'm going back to school."

CHAPTER 14

Beep-beep!

Beep-beep!

"That's our bus," Mr. C. said. "See you tomorrow, Cassie!"

Cassie waved to all her friends. "Bye, Helena! Bye, Mattias! Bye, Lucy! Bye, Seiji! Bye, Arlen! Bye, Laura! Bye, everybody!"

"I'd better get going too," said Sierra. She

grabbed her bike helmet off the hook. "Thanks for inviting me. First grade beats college any day."

Cassie flopped down on the sofa. "Best field trip ever," she said with a happy sigh.

I couldn't agree more. Even Whiskers looked like he'd had fun.

Ding-dong!

"Who could that be?" asked Mom. She opened the front door.

It was Mr. C. He had his clipboard under one arm and Shadow under the other.

"The driver found her on the bus," he said with a smile. "She must have been riding around all day."

Mom thanked Mr. C. and waved good-bye. Shadow scampered behind the sofa.

"Shadow, where have you been?" Cassie said. "And where is your new collar?"

Ding-dong!

"Now who could that be?" Mom asked.

It was Lucky's owner, Mr. Patel.

"Sorry not to call first," he said. "But my conference ended early and I just couldn't wait to get back to Lucky. I hope it's okay if I pick him up today."

"He'll be happy to see you," said Mom. "I'll take you out to him now."

"I'll join you," said Dad.

"Me too," said Cassie. "I want to say hi to Toni."

I smiled. Lucky was going home.

Whiskers jumped up and peered over the back of the sofa. "Shadow!" he scolded. "Where have you been all day?"

Shadow strutted out. "All I can say, Little Brother, is—*best field trip ever.*"

EPILOGUE

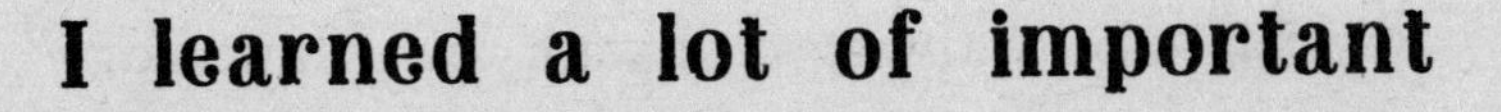

I learned a lot of important lessons from our day with Cassie's class:

1. Lucky's name was a good fit for him after all.
2. Hamsters have snack-packs in their cheeks.
3. It's fun to be part of a school, whether you're a first grader or a fish.
4. Best field trip ever.

The next morning, after Jake, Ethan, and Cassie left for school, Mom and Dad got started on the chores around the inn. Soon Martha arrived to prep the grooming room. Her first customer was . . . *Sheila*?

Sheila had gotten a little too interested in a mud puddle, and was back for another shampoo.

"Hello, cuddly Coco," she whispered. "Nice to see you, wonderful Whiskers. Good morning, darling Dash. Greetings, lovely Leopold. Are you back there, shimmering Shadow? Hi there, beautiful . . . *Blub*? Hey, where's Blub?"

I told her all about Cassie's class visit and how Blub had joined their school. Sheila smiled.

That afternoon, Cassie came home carrying a big thank you card. Her classmates had drawn pictures on it.

"Look, Princess Coco," she said.

There was a drawing of Dash doing a high-five, and one of Leopold taking a bow. There was another of Cassie giving me a big hug, and one of Whiskers on the sofa. There was even a silly drawing of Shadow driving the school bus. Those kids sure had great imaginations.

Cassie opened the card to show me the inside. It said:

Thank you, Animal Inn.

We promise to love your pet as much as you do.

And underneath, there was a photo of Blub, happily swimming with all his new school friends.

FIND OUT WHAT HAPPENS IN THE NEXT **ANIMAL INN** STORY.

Ping-ping!

Lately there's been a lot of "pinging" around here—from Mom's phone, from Dad's phone, and from the computer in the office.

Ping-ping!

Welcome to Animal Inn. My name is Shadow.

I'm what you might call an escape artist. I also happen to be a cat.

No, I'm not one of those silly cats you see in videos on the Internet. That would be my little brother, Whiskers.

I prefer to stay in the shadows. That way it's easier to sneak outside without anyone noticing.

I'm part of the Tyler family. Our family includes five humans—Mom, Dad, Jake, Ethan, and Cassie—and seven animals:

- Me
- Whiskers—my little brother
- Dash—a dog
- Coco—another dog
- Leopold—a bird
- and Fuzzy and Furry—a pair of rodents (Okay, they're technically gerbils.)

We all live together in this old house in the Virginia countryside. Animal Inn is one part hotel, one part school, and one part spa. As our brochure says: *We promise to love your pet as much as you do.*

Ping-ping!

Another message?

It could be a Pekinese in need of a pedicure. A Siamese requesting a short stay. Or a llama in need of a long stay. Once, we even had a Komodo dragon bunk in our basement.

On the first floor of Animal Inn, we have the Welcome Area, the office, the classroom, the grooming room, and the party and play room. The Welcome Area is where you'll find the all-so-important sofa. The sofa is my brother's favorite place to rest, and my favorite place to hide.

Our family lives on the second floor. This is

where you'll find the kitchen, dining room, and bedrooms. You'll also find Fuzzy and Furry in their gerbiltorium in Jake and Ethan's room.

The third floor is for our smaller guests. If you need an aquarium, a terrarium, or a solarium, the third floor is for you. But if you bark, meow, neigh, or bleat, you'll be accommodated out in the barn and kennels.

Ping-ping!

Wow! Animal Inn has gotten so popular lately—famous even. And to think, it all started with Whiskers, a web video, and a big dog.

Let me tell you what happened. . . .

It began like any other Saturday morning at Animal Inn—busy!

On Saturdays, Mom teaches her Polite Puppies class. That's when a herd of little yippers invades the inn. They come to learn some manners. And trust me, they have a lot of work to do.

Dad and Jake also host the Furry Pages. That's when children read aloud to an animal buddy.

Plus, there are grooming appointments and usually a birthday party or two.

Saturday is my favorite day of the week, and not because I'm a big fan of puppies. It's my favorite day because the front door is always opening and closing, giving me plenty of chances to sneak outside.

On this particular morning, my little brother Whiskers was curled up on the sofa in the Welcome Area. Leopold was on his perch, and Dash and Coco were out for a walk with Mom and Cassie.

I was hiding behind the sofa, waiting for things to start hopping when I heard Dad, Jake, and Ethan coming down the stairs. I peeked out to see Ethan carefully holding Dad's smartphone.

"I'll be outside if you need me, boys," said Dad.

"I want to clear the leaves from the walkway before our first guests arrive. I can't wait to try my new leaf blower."

Dad paused before opening the front door and smiled. "I see you hiding back there, Shadow," he said. He quickly opened the door and closed it behind him.

Drat.

"Are you ready, Ethan?" asked Jake.

Ethan held up the smartphone. "I'm ready," he said. "Action!"

"Welcome to Animal Inn," Jake said to the camera. "Here at Animal Inn we promise to love your pet as much as you do. My name is Jake. Today we are going to show you Saturday chores. First on our list, we tidy up the brochures."

"Cut!" said Ethan.

"What's the problem?" asked Jake.

"It doesn't make sense to show brochures in a *web* video," said Ethan.

"Good point," said Jake. "This information is all online anyway. I'll skip that part and go straight to feeding the pets."

"Okay," said Ethan. "Action!"

"Our first morning chore is to feed the Animal Inn pets," said Jake. He walked toward the supply closet.

I slinked out from behind the sofa to see what would be for breakfast.

"Cut!" said Ethan again.

"What now?" asked Jake.

"Everybody knows we feed the pets," said Ethan. "This is supposed to be a really cool video for our website. What's the next chore?"

"Sweeping the Welcome Area," said Jake with a sigh.

"That isn't very exciting," said Ethan.

I looked around. Ethan was right. The Welcome Area wasn't very exciting at the moment. Leopold was preening his feathers, and my little brother Whiskers was already dozing.

"Let's give it one more try," said Jake.

Ethan held up the phone. "Action!" he said.

Urrrrrrrrr!

Dad appeared outside the window with the leaf blower strapped to his back. He wore big safety goggles and ear-protection headphones. Leaves blew all around him.

Urrrrrrrrr!

Whiskers's eyes suddenly shot open.

He spotted the figure at the window and leaped

high into the air, paws stretched straight out in front. He soared in a perfect arc, then landed with a thump and skedaddled up the stairs.

"Wow!" said Jake, turning to the camera. "Now that was exciting!"

"And cut!" said Ethan.

Mermaid Tales
Exciting under-the-sea adventures with
Shelly and her mermaid friends!
Trouble at Trident Academy
Battle of the Best Friends
A Whale of a Tale
Danger in the Deep Blue Sea
The Lost Princess
The Secret Sea Horse
A Royal Tea
The Polar Bear Express
MermaidTalesBooks.com